JN

D0578837

First published in the United States in 1991 by
Ideals Publishing Corporation
Nashville, Tennessee 37210

First published in Great Britain by
Piccadilly Press
London, England

Printed in Hong Kong by South China Printing Company

Library of Congress Cataloging-in-Publication Data

Day, David. 1947-
 The swan children/adapted by David Day; illustrated by
Richard Evans.
  p. cm.
 Summary: The Magician King's four grandchildren are
transformed into swans by their jealous stepmother and
remain enchanted for a thousand years.
 ISBN 0-8249-8461-7
 [1. Fairy tales. 2. Folklore—Ireland.] I. Evans, Richard,
1954- ill. II. Title.
PZ8.D244Su   1991
398.2—dc20
[E]   91-10007
                                                         CIP
                                                          AC

The Swan Children

adapted by David Day

illustrated by Richard Evans

Ideals Children's Books • Nashville, Tennessee

For Jane Laura Smith
- D.D.

For all my family
- R.E.

In the days of dragons and unicorns, in the ancient land of Ireland, there lived a magical tribe called the Tuatha dé Danaan. They were a radiantly beautiful people who were both wise and strong.

Of all the tribe, the most famous was King Lir, who had once ruled over a magical underwater kingdom of the dé Danaan called the Land-Beneath-the-Waves, far below the Western Sea. When this mighty Sea King came to Ireland, he built a magnificent, gold-roofed palace, the finest in all the land.

Lir was the happiest of men. He was the richest of kings, his lands were peaceful and prosperous, and his wife was the most beautiful queen in Ireland.

Lir's queen was called Naomi, and she was the blue-eyed, honey-haired daughter of Redbeard, the powerful Magician King of Galway.

Soon after their marriage, Lir and Naomi were blessed with two children: a daughter called Finola and a son called Aedi. Finola was as fair and gentle as her mother, and Aedi was as handsome and strong as his father.

As time passed, two more children were born. These were the twin brothers Fiachra and Conn. Both were strong and healthy, but after their birth, a terrible tragedy befell this royal family.

Queen Naomi suffered a long illness. Life slowly faded from her, and she died.

King Lir grieved over the loss of his queen. It was only the love of his four children that consoled him. Often the children would sing sweetly and cheer him with their delicate voices.

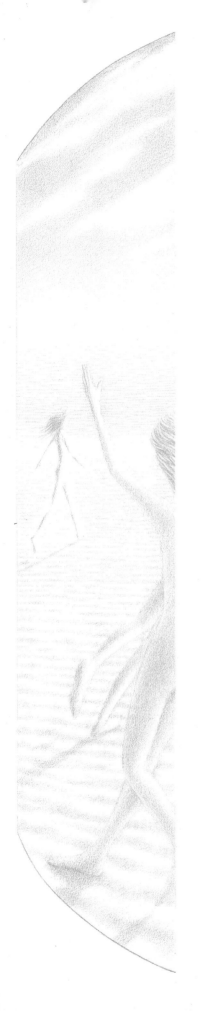

The children of Lir possessed the finest voices in the land. Nobility from all over Ireland came to Lir's court just to hear the children's healing songs.

As time passed, Lir's grief became less, and he saw that his children once again needed a woman's guiding hand. Naomi's sister, the beautiful princess Ava, came to the palace to care for her niece and nephews.

Although Lir would never forget Naomi, he soon came to love this dark-haired, green-eyed princess. In every way, Ava seemed as good and kind as her sister had been. Equal, too, had been these sisters in the casting of spells and enchantments, for both were daughters of Redbeard the Magician King.

So, at last, Lir proclaimed that there would be a royal wedding. Lir's children happily accepted their loving aunt as their stepmother, and all the lords and ladies of Ireland came to the grand wedding feast to welcome Ava as their new queen.

All seemed well again in Lir's kingdom.
Yet, after the wedding feast, an old woman
came secretly to speak with the children. This
old woman had been their mother's childhood
nurse, and she had been at Queen Naomi's side
during her last hours.

The old woman had been given a small, silver box
by the children's mother. This box was to be given to
the children should the king ever marry again.

Within the box were four silver chain necklaces.

Each was set with a single pure-white stone.
The children were delighted with these gifts.
Thanking the old nurse, the children took
their necklaces and promised to wear
them always.

For a time, there was great happiness in the royal palace. The children grew sturdy and tall, and their singing became lovelier and more skilled each year. Yet more than anything else in the world, Ava wished to have children of her own. However, no matter how much she longed for them, Queen Ava remained childless.

Ava's loving nature gradually changed. Although still beautiful, the queen became a sad, bitter woman.

She brooded and grieved for the children she could never have until her thoughts bothered her both day and night, like a terrible sickness. As time passed, Ava's bitterness with her fate turned her against the children of Lir.

Ava became jealous of their beauty, of their talent, and even of Lir's love for them. The children, in turn, became disturbed and confused by this change in their stepmother.

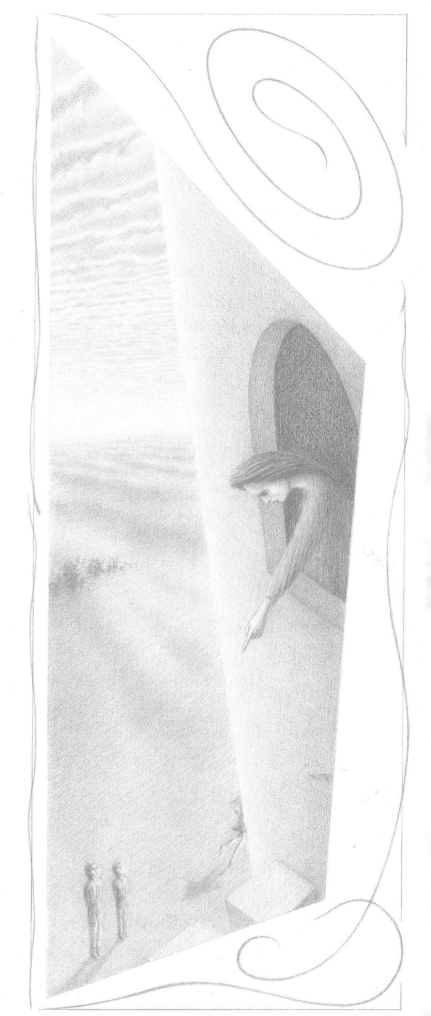

Miraculously one morning, after many long months of unhappiness, Ava appeared to be suddenly cured of the bitter sickness. Once more there was joy and laughter in the palace, and the family seemed happy and well.

One fine summer's day, Ava and the four children set out on a journey to visit Redbeard. After traveling for many miles, they came to the shimmering water of Lake Darvra. The day was hot, and the lake was clear and cool, so Ava suggested that they might rest awhile.

The children were delighted. They threw their clothes down on the shore and leaped into the lake. Although the clear, deep water refreshed her as she swam, Finola soon felt a fearful pounding in her chest.

Something was wrong. Conn, Aedi, and Fiachra felt it too. It was a voice—not loud, but powerful and strange. It was pulsing and shuddering even in the deepest parts of the lake.

It was Ava calling from the shore. She was calling in a way that was both terrifying to hear and impossible not to obey. And although the frightened children wished to hide deep in the lake, they were pulled toward the shore by the queen's commanding powers.

Ava's green eyes were blazing, and her wild, black hair seemed to float in the air. Finola suddenly realized that the bitter sickness had not left at all—Ava simply hid her hatred so she might lure them to this place.

Deep in a trance, Ava's hard, straight lips were barely moving as she chanted the strange words of the dreadful spell over and over again.

Finola cried out in pain and, with her brothers, begged Ava to stop. But as Finola raised her arms from the water, she saw long, white feathers had grown from them. She swept her arms back and forth in shock. Her arms had become wings!

She looked frantically at her three brothers. They were changing. White feathers began to cover all of them. Their necks grew long, their bodies became squat, their feet were webbed. They were all becoming swans!

Satisfied with her evil work, the queen mounted her chariot and fled Lake Darvra as the terrified swan children struggled in fear and confusion on its shore. When Ava arrived at Redbeard's castle, she pretended to be insane with grief.

She had torn her clothes and scratched her cheeks, and she told all within the court a woeful tale of how she and the children had been set upon by wild beasts. So fierce and sudden was the attack that, despite all she could do, the children were killed and dragged away by the monsters.

However, the queen's evil plan had not worked as perfectly as she had imagined. Nor did the powers of her enchantment go entirely unchallenged when she cast her vicious spell. For the enchantress knew nothing of those four charmed necklaces which her sister had left for the children. The magical power of the necklaces had allowed the children to keep their human voices.

Within days of the evil deed, travelers came to Redbeard's castle to tell the strange tale of four miraculous swans at Lake Darvra who sang with voices of human children. It did not take long for the king to learn the true fate of his lost grandchildren.

In all Ireland, none possessed greater magical powers than Redbeard. And even though Ava was his own beloved daughter, it was his duty to find a just punishment for his daughter's crime.

Calling upon the deepest powers of the earth, Redbeard's fiery eyes blazed as he began to chant a terrible spell. The frightened Ava was unable to move or cry out as a whirling column of smoke and mist swept around her. Slowly, the whirlwind rose up from the floor and vanished into the air.

The beautiful queen was gone and in her place was a solitary black egg.

As all the court looked on, the egg cracked and a silver-white vapor seeped out through the opening in the shell. The vapor rose higher and formed a small, glowing cloud.

Then the egg cracked wider and an ugly black rat leaped out.

The Magician King had split his daughter's spirit into two parts. All that was good emerged from the egg as the pure spirit of that small, glowing cloud. All that was evil emerged in the form of that spiteful black rat.

The little beast squealed angrily at the king, but as suddenly as it appeared, so did the court cat. The rat fled.

As the rat vanished through a crack in the wall, the glowing cloud drifted across the room and went out through a window. The rat had been condemned to scramble and creep forever in fearful darkness, while the little cloud would wander eternally in the world in light and freedom.

Although Ava's punishment was just and the power of the Magician King was great, he could not undo his daughter's spell.

Much to Lir's sorrow, his children remained trapped within the bodies of swans. Furthermore, the evil spell bound them for three full centuries to the waters of Lake Darvra.

Rather than allow his children to live apart from him, King Lir abandoned his own palace. On the shores of Darvra, Lir built a new city so that he and his people might live within the sight and sound of his beloved children.

Those three centuries spent on the lake were not unhappy years. The swan children remained forever young, and as time passed, they became very wise. Their singing became more refined, filled with deep knowledge and great joy.

One morning, Finola awoke early and roused her brothers. The time had come for them to leave the lake. The swans flew up into the air, singing and circling around the towers of the city.

The dé Danaan came out into the streets. They called the swans by name and pleaded with them to stay awhile longer. But nothing could be done.

After three long centuries, the swan children's trials had only begun. The evil spell now compelled them to fly into a lonely exile on that treacherous sea to the north of Ireland, the Sea of Moyle.

Upon the storm-tossed and wintry
sea, the swan children made their home.
At times it became solid with ice and froze
their feathers to its surface. At other times, great
waves beat upon them as they struggled to survive.
Yet they did survive, and another three terrible
centuries passed. But this did not bring their torment to
an end, for the children of Lir were once again compelled to
fly to a new place of exile. This was called the Western Sea, and
although this sea was not so bitter-cold, it storms were often greater
as they broke upon Ireland's western shore.

So, when at long last,
the span of three times three centuries
had come to an end, Finola and her brothers let out a shout
of joy. The grip of the evil spell no longer bound them to one place,
but allowed them to fly wherever they wished.

Joyfully, they flew at once to seek out the dé Danaan. And though
the children of Lir flew over the length and width of Ireland, they
found only a ruined castle and its broken towers to mark the place
where the ancient kingdom once stood. Slowly, the children came to
understand that they were now the last of the dé Danaan upon the
face of the earth.

After much wandering
in sorrow, the enchanted children came
to settle in the calm, sheltered waters of Innis Gloire.
This became their home. The fishermen and seafarers of the west
spoke with pride of the magical singing swans of the Isle of Gloire.

A thousand years after that evil queen's spell was cast, a strange man in a black robe came to Innis Gloire. Neither the swans nor any of the island people had ever seen his like before. He was a holy man, a black-robed priest who spoke of the coming of a new god.

The swan children watched as the priest built a chapel and bell tower. They watched in silence as the tower rose, stone by stone, higher and higher.

At last the tower was completed, and the priest put a great iron bell in the tower. On that day, all the people of Gloire were gathered before the chapel and bell tower. And just as the sun rose in the morning sky, the swan children came as well, and they began to sing.

This was the sweetest song that has ever been sung upon the earth in all time. Ecstatic and sorrowful at once, their singing filled the air with a thousand years of enchantments and glories of ancient Ireland. And all those who had come to hear the bell in the tower immediately forgot why they had come.

All except the priest were captivated by those voices. The priest stood silently at the foot of the tower. Then he pulled the bell's cord. The iron bell rang out from the tower—loud and strong.

In that moment, a miracle happened. As the bell rang out, the silver chains around the swans' necks burst apart, and Finola and her brothers trembled like the bell itself.

Their shimmering feathers began to fall from their bodies. Their wings became arms, their webbed feet became human.

The tolling bell rang out the age of enchantment. The power of ancient spells and curses vanished. A new age had been rung in.

Before the chapel there stood the four children of Lir—glittering, magical beings as young and beautiful as they had been a thousand years before.

Finola, Aedi, Fiachra, and Conn were amazed. At last—after ten centuries—the evil spell had been lifted!

Yet, the children knew at once that their freedom would have its price. The iron bell had rung in a new age. They were children of a lost time and a lost race. They could not survive within this new world.

So, as the bell tolled, the children of Lir turned away from the tower and the people, and walked toward the sea. The bell rang as the children stepped into the water. It rang as they waded waist-deep into the sea. It rang once again as the water washed over their heads and the children disappeared.

The children swam far and deep beneath the surface of the sea to that most ancient Land-Beneath-the-Waves. They rejoiced to find that their father—and all the dé Danaan with him—had returned to the undersea kingdom.

It is a magical realm that exists still. And there, Lir the Sea King rules from his palace. In his throne room, he is attended by mermaids and sea-unicorns. His lords and ladies still have great feasts and festivals.

And best of all—once again and forevermore—he hears the angelic voices of his children resound throughout the great halls of his palace.